The Island-below-the-Star

written and illustrated by James Rumford

Houghton Mifflin Company
Boston   1998

The text of this book is set in Monotype Bulmer.
Hawaiian accents for Monotype Bulmer designed by Hans Loffel.
The illustrations are done in watercolor on Arches paper.

Library of Congress Cataloging-in-Publication Data
Rumford, James.
   The island-below-the-star / written and illustrated by James Rumford.
      p.   cm.
   Summary: Five brothers, each with a special skill, sail across the
vast Pacific Ocean to the islands now known as Hawaii.
   ISBN 0-395-85159-9
   [1. Voyages and travels—Fiction. 2. Brothers—Fiction.
3. Hawaii—Discovery and exploration—Fiction.] I. Title.
PZ7.R8878Is   1998   97-9568
[Fic]—dc21   CIP
                        AC

Printed in Singapore
TWP 10 9 8 7 6 5 4 3 2 1

To my wife and son

In the days when the stars were a map of the earth below, there lived on a tiny island in the South Pacific five brothers who loved adventure. The first brother was Hōkū, and he loved the sun, the moon, and especially the stars.

The second was Nāʻale, and he loved the sea.
The third was ʻŌpua, and he loved clouds.
The fourth was Makani, and he loved the wind.
And the fifth was tiny Manu, and he loved birds.

One night, Hōkū said, "See, my brothers, that bright star there? There's an island below that star. Let us sail to it."

And as he spoke, the star sparkled with adventure.

Hōkū's four brothers looked up at the star over their own island and saw how very far away the other star was. No one had ever gone so far before.

Little Manu was first to speak. "I will go with you, Hōkū."

The other brothers, including Hōkū, laughed. Such a dangerous trip was out of the question for such a little boy.

"You might get washed overboard," said Nā'ale.

"Or frightened by the thunder and lightning," said 'Ōpua.

"Or blown away by the wind," said Makani. "Besides, you only care about birds."

The next morning, Manu stood watching as his four brothers prepared for their great trip without him to the Island-below-the-Star.

Hōkū dried bananas, taro, and breadfruit in the hot sun, for they would need much food.

Nā'ale fashioned dozens of fishhooks and readied the harpoons,

for they would live off the sea as well.

'Ōpua watched the clouds and gathered only the sweetest rainwater, for they would be thirsty on their long trip.

Makani repaired the sails, for they would need to catch even the tiniest breeze if they were ever to reach the Island-below-the-Star.

After several weeks, the canoe was seaworthy and the food and water were loaded on board. There was a great celebration for the four brothers.

Little Manu did not join in. No one noticed as he hid himself among the calabashes of food and baskets of coconuts.

The brothers left just before dawn.

It was sunset before they discovered little Manu.

"Let's toss him overboard and let him swim back," said Nāʻale.

"Let's throw him into the air and let the wind carry him home," said Makani.

Big ʻŌpua picked Manu up and held him over the side of the canoe.

"Hōkū!" cried Manu with his arms outstretched. "Hōkū!"

"All right! All right!" shouted ʻŌpua. "We were just kidding."

Hōkū began to laugh. "But you had better behave yourself," he told Manu.

Manu stood there, his head down.

"Make yourself useful," said Nāʻale. "We need fish."

Several weeks later, it was Makani who first noticed a strange rush of warm air. He scanned the horizon.

The waves began to grow in strength as they slapped against the hull. Nāʻale alerted the others.

A thin palm frond of a cloud appeared above the horizon. ʻŌpua prepared his brothers for the worst.

By evening, the sky that Hōkū depended on was roiling with clouds.
The waves were mountains. The wind was a knife.

The brothers tied a safety rope to Manu.
For five days and nights they hung on for dear life as they rode out the storm.

At last, the wind died down. The sea was calm, but the sky was still hidden behind a gray blanket of clouds. The canoe had been blown far off course. The brothers were lost.

Manu undid the safety rope. He had not cried when the thunder crashed through the sky. He had not been washed overboard or carried off by the wind.

Suddenly Manu stood very still. He could feel something coming.

He looked up and saw, perhaps on its way to the Island-below-the-Star, a tiny speck of a bird.

Manu called to his brothers, "Look, brothers, a bird! A bird on its way to land!"

"Where?" they cried. It was so high that they could not see it.

"Tell me where it is, Manu," said Hōkū. "Tell me which way to go."

Manu pointed in the direction the bird was flying, and Hōkū turned the canoe.

The bird stayed with the brothers all through the day, and Manu, proud Manu, told Hōkū of the bird's every turn.

That night, when the skies finally cleared, they all saw that they were beneath their star.

But where was the island?

Nā'ale showed them the waves crashing into one another, as though pushed back by something big.

'Ōpua pointed to the moonlit clouds gathered in the north as though caught by a mountain.

Makani told them how the wind was swirling oddly, as though avoiding some huge shape.

No one slept.

Manu, now part of the team, spotted the first birds in the predawn light.

They were close—very close.

And then, at dawn, they saw the island. Its peaks
towered above the waves and caught the first rays

of the rising sun. The brothers shouted with
joy and lifted Manu high on their shoulders.

At noon, they found a quiet bay for the canoe.

At sunset, they set foot on shore.

That night, they gave thanks for their safe journey as they stood directly below the bright star that had called to them.

In the days when the stars were islands floating in a dark,
heavenly sea and people were explorers living on specks of
land surrounded by the vast ocean, they sang of
Hōkū, the star,

Nā'ale, the ocean waves,
'Ōpua, the cloud bank,
Makani, the wind, and
Manu, the bird, who found the Island-below-the-Star.

Note

This story tells how, more than 1,500 years ago, early Polynesian explorers discovered the islands below the star Arcturus. These islands are known today as the Hawaiian Islands. The explorers are believed to have come from the Marquesas Islands, 2,500 miles to the south. Later they would return south to bring their families to the new land.

When people came to the Pacific Ocean thousands and thousands of years ago, they slowly learned its ways. They studied sea currents and winds. They studied the night sky and the ocean storms. And they studied the migration of birds. This knowledge helped them cross the vast ocean without maps, compasses, or satellites.

No one knows what pushed the Pacific peoples to explore the ocean and colonize its islands. Perhaps they were searching for food in times of famine. Perhaps they wished to escape an evil ruler. Or perhaps, as in this story, they longed to explore.

For the past twenty years, people all over the Pacific have been rediscovering the ancient art of wayfinding. They have built the canoes of their ancestors, studied the starry skies, and learned again the songs of the wind, the rhythms of the ocean, and the migratory patterns of birds. In this way, they have retraced ancient sea routes and given new voice to the chants of the brave navigators of old.